HERE LIES
THE BODY
of
JEREMY VICTOR.

HE SHOULDN'T
HAVE HUGGED
HIS
BOA CONSTRICTOR.

———

SLEEP TIGHT.

Henry Holt and Company, Inc.
Publishers since 1866
115 West 18th Street
New York, New York 10011

Henry Holt is a registered
trademark of Henry Holt and Company, Inc.

Text copyright © 1999 by Joan Horton
Illustrations copyright © 1999 by JoAnn Adinolfi
All rights reserved.
Published in Canada by Fitzhenry & Whiteside Ltd.,
195 Allstate Parkway, Markham, Ontario L3R 4T8.

Library of Congress Cataloging-in-Publication Data
Horton, Joan.
Halloween hoots and howls / by Joan Horton;
illustrated by JoAnn Adinolfi.
Summary: A collection of poems celebrating
Halloween, including "Tombstone Epitaph," "The
Ghost and Goblin Ball," and "The Vampire."
1. Halloween—Juvenile poetry. 2. Children's
poetry, American. [1. Halloween—Poetry.
2. American poetry.] 1. Adinolfi, JoAnn, ill. II. Title.
PS3558.O6984H35 1999 811.54—dc21 98-43346

ISBN 0-8050-5805-2 / First Edition—1999

The artist used gouache, water colors, and pastels to create
the illustrations for this book. Designed by Martha Rago.
Printed in the United States of America on acid-free paper. ∞

1 3 5 7 9 10 8 6 4 2

For
Ken,
with
love
—J. H.

For
Brother and
Donna,
Halloween
revelers. Boo!
—J. A.

HALLOWEEN
Hoots and Howls

Joan Horton

ILLUSTRATED BY

JoAnn Adinolfi

Henry Holt and Company

NEW YORK

I'm dressing up for Halloween—
Don't want to be a bat,
A mummy, ghost, or skeleton,
Or a witch's snarling cat.
Don't want to be a werewolf
With hairy hands and face;
Instead I'll be an alien
Beamed down from outer space—
A creature with antennae
And a green-and-purple hide,
But best of all, a creature
With three arms on either side.
Six arms for hanging bags on
Before I hit the street;
Just think of all the loot I'll get
Tonight for trick or treat.

WOE IS ME

"Woe is me," the pumpkin said.

"They plucked me from my garden bed,

Hollowed all my innards out,

And with a joyful whoop and shout,

Carved two eyes, a nose, a grin,

And stuck a lighted candle in.

Next they set me on a post

Where every goblin, ghoul, and ghost,

Howling, prowling through the night,

Filled my orange skull with fright.

As if that wasn't bad enough,"

The pumpkin grumbled in a huff,

"They later baked me in a pie,

And now they're eating me—G O O D - B Y E!"

THE GHOST AND GOBLIN BALL

There's going to be a party.
We've rented out the hall.
You're invited to be present
At the Ghost and Goblin Ball.

There'll be rockin' to the rhythm
Of the Clicking Clacking Bones
As the skeletons play backup
To the screeching of The Crones.

Little cocktail hallow-wieners
And a sparkling witch's brew
Will be served throughout the evening
By a frightful phantom crew.

And at the stroke of midnight,
In the dankest of the rooms,
Guests will feast on lizard gizzards
And entrails robbed from tombs.

There's going to be a party.
You're invited one and all.
We'll be waiting there to greet you
At the Ghost and Goblin Ball.

I FLY THROUGH THE AIR

I fly through the air

With the greatest of ease,

Just like the man on the flying trapeze.

I dive and I swoop in my spotlight, the moon;

These daredevil antics make young witches swoon.

I hang by my toes without even a mat.

Come see me perform—I'm The Great Acro-BAT.

THE VAMPIRE

One waking vampire rising from his tomb.

One thirsty vampire stalking through the gloom.

Sharp fangs gleaming white,

Looking for a neck to bite,

While you're fast asleep at night,

He's searching for your room.

THEY PUT HIM IN A COFFIN

They put him in a coffin

And nailed the lid down tight.

But if you happen by his grave

Some wild and stormy night,

You're apt to see a hand crawl out

And beckon you draw near.

But best beware, for if you dare,

You'll surely disappear.

WHEN A SKELETON GETS CREAKY

When a skeleton gets creaky
And complains of aching bones
Or a haunt gets fits of hacking
Each and every time he moans,
He goes to see the witch doctor,
Who writes him a prescription
For liniment and coffin syrup
Concocted in her kitchen.

WITCH HAZEL BRAND

BEING A SKELETON ISN'T SO EASY

Being a skeleton isn't so easy.

When wintertime comes and the weather gets freezy.

It shivers my bones from my front to my back;

I shake and I rattle, click clickety-clack.

Click clickety-clack, clack clackety-click,

Somebody throw me an overcoat—quick!

AGGIE WITCH'S ADS

FOR SALE:

Broomstick for sale—
Low mileage, very clean,
Flown once a year on Halloween.
Imported handle, splinter-free.
With room for cat. Must see!
Call A. Witch.

WANTED:

Turbo broomstick (color—jet)
With dual exhausts, FM cassette,
Cruise control plus radar screen
For spotting bats on Halloween.
Call A. Witch.
(Leave message on answering machine.)

ME

MY DOG

X RAY

"This is your X ray,"

Said young Doctor Jones

As he held up a picture

That showed me my bones.

My eyes opened wide

At this curious sight.

It looks like I'm ready

For Halloween night.

THE DANCING GHOST

He wins prizes for dancing the tango,
The rumba, the waltz, and fandango.
He heads up the line for the conga;
No one's better at dancing the samba.
He can leap through the air in ballet,
Even disco the whole night away.
He taps out a rhythm, not missing a beat,
But how does he do it without any feet?

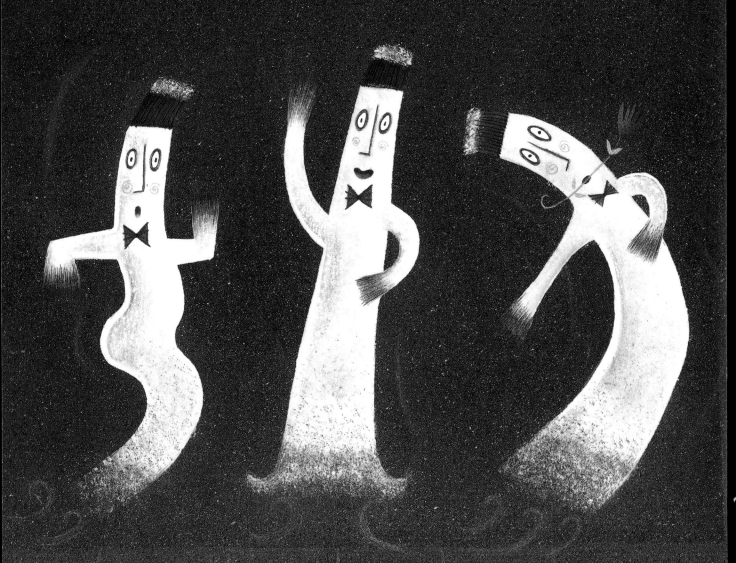

THE SCAREDY-CAT GHOST

I'm a ghost who's afraid of walking through walls;
I shiver and shake when a hoot owl calls.
I start at the sounds of the things that go bump;
My very own shadow would cause me to jump.
A tap at the window or creak on the stair
Sends me diving for cover—though nobody's there.
I'm a scaredy-cat ghost, I've been one since YOU
Crept up behind me and shouted out BOO!

A HALLOWEENY QUIZ

Here's a Halloweeny quiz.
Score ten points and you're a whiz.
Grab a pencil, have some fun,
Then figure out how well you've done.

1 What streets do ghosts haunt when they're out with their friends?
SCORE A POINT IF YOU SAID "DEAD ENDS."

2 Which little witch does the teacher like best?
THE ONE WITH AN "A" ON HER LAST SPELL-ING TEST.

3 Where do vampires keep all of their cash?
THE BLOOD BANK'S THE PLACE WHERE THEIR MONEY IS STASHED.

4 What games do ghosts play in the dead of the night?
IF YOU SAID "HIDE-AND-SHRIEK," THAT'S ANOTHER ONE RIGHT.

5 Why do skeletons hide all their brooms?
SO THE LAZYBONES WON'T HAVE TO CLEAN THEIR ROOMS.

6 What do vampires most like to eat?
NECK-TARINES ARE THEIR FAVORITE TREATS.

7 When the corpse got a cold, do you know what he said?
"I FEEL ROTTEN AND THINK THAT I'LL STAY HOME IN BED."

8 Who did the vampire take on a date?
HIS GHOUL-FRIEND, OF COURSE. (DOES YOUR SCORE TOTAL EIGHT?)

9 What kind of breakfast does Frankenstein eat?
SCRAMBLED LEGS WITH GHOST TOASTIES AND HOT SCREAM OF WHEAT.

10 What did the werewolf say to the owl?
THE JOKES IN THIS QUIZ ARE A HOOT AND A HOWL.

IGOR'S MUMMY

Igor's mummy drives the bus

That takes the kids to school.

Boys and ghouls who ride with her

Must always mind this rule:

No throwing things or hitting,

Or making any fuss,

And screaming hyenas had better behave

Or else get off the bus.

WITCH HAZEL'S DINER MENU

Electric eels,
thinly sliced

Baby bat wings,
hotly spiced

Worms in brine
(cup or bowl)

Dragon entrails casserole

Sumac salad, green and chivey,
tossed with lots of poison ivy

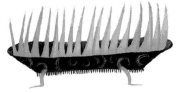

Spider bundt cake

Witches' Brew
(regular and decaf, too)

RECIPE FOR GOBLIN PUNCH

In a cauldron or a pot,

Mix and heat till bubbling hot:

Six cups of water from a sluice,

Three cans of frozen orange juice,

One-quarter teaspoon nutmeg, ground,

One hoot of owl, one bay of hound,

Two teaspoonfuls of ginger spice

(Chant a spell while stirring twice).

Add lemon juice, one tablespoon,

As yellow as a witch's moon,

Plus a quart of ghoulish cider,

Pour and top with hairy spider.

NO ONE WILL DARE-DOUBLE-DARE TRICK-OR-TREAT

No one will dare-double-dare trick-or-treat

At that tumbledown house at the end of the street.

Not since that Halloween night long ago

When the moon rode high and the wind moaned low.

That's when a boy in a ghost-white sheet

Lifted the knocker and cried, "Trick or treat!"

But while he stood waiting, he wasn't aware

Someone or something was lurking in there.

Then an old hag with a wart on her chin

Creaked open the door and beckoned him in.

As soon as the boy stepped into the room

He spotted the tall pointed hat and the broom.

It was too late to run; he had no place to hide—

The grinning old witch hovered close by his side.

Then she shrieked and she cackled and waggled her head,

"I love trick-or-treaters," she wickedly said.

"But the trick is on *you*, my delectable sweet."

And she gobbled him up for her Halloween treat.

Doctor Frankenstein went to the market
And stopped in the vegetable aisle.
He picked up a firm head of cabbage
And moved on with a sly little smile.

"Potatoes with eyes should do nicely,"
The doctor said, stroking his chin.
"And so will these two ears of corn
That are here in the very next bin."

The wheels on his shopping cart squeaked
As he pushed it down aisle number three
And found elbow and angel-hair pasta
Just where he thought they would be.

Next on his list were bananas.
"Two hands will most certainly do."
As he headed right for the fruit stand,
He saw them with five fingers, too.

When Frankenstein stopped at the meat case,
The sight set his body aquiver,
For there, behind glass, were two kidneys,
A brain, a heart, and a liver.

"I'll take them," he said to the butcher.
But his shopping was still not complete.
So he asked him for two legs of lamb,
Some ribs, and a pair of pig's feet.

He hurried straight home with his bundles
And crept down the stairs to his lab.
He unpacked them with care on his work space,
A seven-foot-long marble slab.

His eyes were ablaze with excitement
At the thought of the thing he would make.
He worked through the night without stopping,
Till dawn was beginning to break.

And when he was finally finished,
He tingled with glee for he knew
That this was his finest creation—
A savory, succulent stew.

Well, what did you think he would do?

THERE'S A SPIDER ON THE CEILING

There's a spider on the ceiling,
There's a spider on the floor;
There's a spider in the corner
That was never there before.
There's a spider on the curtain;
One is dangling from a web,
And I have a creepy feeling
One is crawling in my bed.
Now a spider's on my pillow;
There are spiders circling round,
If I listen very closely,
I can hear a whirring sound.
For they all have started spinning
Sticky strands to wrap their prey;
They want me for a midnight snack,
I'm out of here—GANGWAY!

BEDTIME

Hurry, hurry! Cover your head;

Ghoulies and ghosties hide under your bed.

Quickly, quickly! Pull in your feet;

You never can tell what these beasties might eat.

Listen, listen! Don't make a sound;

They're thumping and bumping and looking around.

If you curl up and make yourself small,

Maybe they'll never find you at all.

But if they do, yell for your mother—

Or, even better, feed them your brother!